Eleanor Fitzgerald

Hymns for the Gallows

Volume Two: The Last Meal

An anthology of works by Eleanor Fitzgerald

Hymns For The Gallows Volume Two

First paperback edition March 2021

ISBN: 9798712286690
Published Independently

Eleanor Fitzgerald

For Anna,
Because you're hella cute, hella gay, and we were steamed hams
together.

Table of Contents

A Note from the Writer

I'd like to add a **Content Warning** for, among other things, blood, medical interventions, discussions of suicide, and abuse throughout this anthology.

Once again, the words contained within these pages are inspired by dreams I've had, experiences I've lived, and the way other pieces of art made me feel.

Poetry is, in my opinion, a much more dangerous art form than a novel; far more of your soul bleeds through on to the page. These stories and poems blur the line between Dark and Eleanor, and whilst I am happy for you to know the heart of me, the details of my life are mine and mine alone. I know it's human nature to speculate and that asking you to refrain is requesting the impossible, but I'm going to ask all the same.

I appreciate your discretion.

Thank you.

Part One: Entrée

<u>Entrée</u>

"You want to know what kind of person thinks about food at a time like this?" The Prison Officer is a short older man, with wispy hair and dark eyes. His voice, however, is kind.

Dark nods through her tears.

"People who accept what is coming and want to enjoy what few pleasures they have left." Dark scoffs. "Is that really so awful? I've seen a lot of people pass through here over the years, most of them poor, most of them *different* in one way or another, and I'll tell you what I've always told them.

"This meal is the most liberating meal you will ever eat. You don't need to worry about how much it costs, you don't need to worry about doing the dishes, and you certainly don't need to worry about the health ramifications. You can eat whatever you like and however much of it you want, and be damned the consequences.

"You've got all night too, so make sure you have the full three courses you're allocated and take your time to enjoy them. The rules say you're supposed to be left on your own until they come for you in the morning, but that just doesn't seem decent to me. If you'd rather be alone, then I will absolutely leave you be, but if not I'll be here, right up until the very end; it's the least anyone deserves, no matter what they've done."

"How are most people," Dark asks quietly, "when they come for them?"

"I won't lie, some people react badly and get violent. Most, however, are calm as a summer evening. Most are ready."

Dark takes a moment to dry her eyes and wipe away the tears before relaying her meal request to the Prison Officer. He nods as he jots down her wishes, and passes them outside the cell to one of his colleagues.

"I must say I'm a little surprised at how quickly you made your decision; most people deliberate for almost an hour!"

"My grandfather and I always used to talk about stuff like this," Dark says quietly. "Last meal, desert island books, last film in existence; we spoke about it almost every time we saw each other."

The two sit in silence for a while, until the rattle of trolley breaks through the spell of the moment. The door clangs open and a steaming bowl of matzo ball soup, with a side of latkes and sour cream are placed on the table before Dark.

She leans over the bowl and breathes deeply, a smile crossing her face.

"Good choice." The Prison Officer smiles at her. "Please don't stand on ceremony; tuck in."

Dark begins with a latke, loading it up with sour cream. Her eyes close as she takes the first bite, and a broad grin spreads across her lips.

"You've got a little bit of sour cream," says the Prison Officer, gesturing to the corner of his mouth. Dark's tongue dashes out to deal with the rogue splodge of dairy. "How's the food?"

"It's really good, thank you." Dark ponders for a moment over another mouthful. "You know, I didn't believe you about this being a liberating meal, but I'm already starting to feel a little bit better.

"I guess it's just a bit surreal for me, you know? My transition was literally the only possible way for me to keep on living a life that wasn't continual hell, and I'm being put to death. It's certainly ironic, isn't it?"

"That it is, Dark, that it is."

"Do you mind if I ask your name? I'd feel weird if I didn't know the name of the person I spent the last evening of my life with. I hope that's okay?"

"That's completely fine by me, Dark. My name is Edgar, and I use he/him pronouns, in case you were wondering about that too."

"Most folks don't give their pronouns without a little prodding."

"As I said, I've had all sorts through here. Most didn't deserve the rope, but a few did."

"And those who didn't deserve it, why didn't you help them escape?"

"Oh, I absolutely would if I could. I've been through maybe a hundred different versions of a plan, and not a damn one would work. This place is locked up tighter than a drum, unfortunately.

"It breaks my heart to see such good people put to death."

"Then why not leave? Why stay here?"

"I can't leave, Dark, no matter how much it hurts me. I've been doing this job almost forty years now, and I'll keep doing it until they force me out or death takes me."

"I still don't understand why you can't leave, especially if it hurts as much as you say it does."

"I'm the last person everyone in here gets to speak to, and I mean properly speak to, before they die. That's an important job and I feel that it should be done by someone who cares about all of you.

"Someone kind."

The silence hangs in the air as Dark eats.

Then, after a while, Dark speaks.

"Thank you, Edgar."

"No need to thank me; nobody should face the end alone."

Dark continues eating for a while, making appreciative noises as she does so. After some time passes, she finishes and settles back in her chair.

"Feel free to have a nap if you want, I'm not going to stop

you."

"Do people often sleep?"

"Some do. I don't think they can bear the waiting, which I don't envy them. Most just end up eating their dinner and chatting to me. As I said earlier, if you'd like some space-"

"No, no. Please, I'd rather spend my final hours talking with someone friendly. What do they normally talk about?"

"It varies, at least to start with, but they tend to end up telling me about themselves and their lives."

"I guess it's one way to ensure that you're remembered."

"That it is. When I go home, I write down as much of what I've been told as I can. I try to read through all the notebooks at least once a year. By God, I try to keep those people alive the only way I can."

"Well, I guess I should start at the beginning then.

"I realised I was transgender in my early teens, but I waited until university to really do anything about it. I was so terrified that I was crazy or broken in some way, when in fact I was just different.

"I used to spend so much of my time just daydreaming about how much happier I'd be as a woman, rather than some ungainly boy. I used to wish that I would wake up as I imagined myself in my head, but it never worked out that way.

"I cried myself to sleep most nights. I stopped wishing to be a woman and started wishing for death instead. I didn't want to go through life feeling so out of sorts and incomplete; that's no way to live, Edgar."

"No, no it's not." Edgar's voice is soft and subdued.

"It was only when I got to university that I realised that trans people actually existed and that I wasn't alone. It was a watershed moment and I was never the same.

"The wishing for death was dialled back and the daydreaming

5

started again. I spent so long dreaming about how comfortable in my own skin I'd be if only I were a woman.

"And then one day, almost out of nowhere, a little voice in my brain said 'Hey, that's something you can actually do'."

"Oh?" Edgar smiles. "Was that it then? The moment you started working towards your transition?"

"Hell no, I tried to drink myself to death that night rather than face up to my own transness. It took me a further two years to finally come out."

Dark sighs heavily and holds her head in her hands.

"I wasted so much time on fear, Edgar. So long spent worrying what other people would think that I wasted almost a decade of my life.

"I'd give anything to get those wasted years back."

<u>The Hyena</u>

I'm a scavenger of smiles,
The raggedy opportunist of careless jokes.
Quick with a grin,
Quicker with a laugh.
A solitary pack hunter
Slinking from group to group,
Always hungry for more.
Ever asking
"What are we laughing at?"
A glutton for surrealism,
Starved for satire.
Content with contextless chuckles.
Have you ever notice that people like me
Don't like observational comedy?
A mottled scavenger,
No topic off limits;
The darker the better.
A gift,
My curse,
The struggle to chain the beast.
To reign it in.
My mind is a boneyard of abandoned jokes.
Private humour to pick and pull
At my languid leisure.
My last words will likely mean nothing to the many,
But riotous to the few.

Ere go I, carefully concealed,
Behind my wolfish grin
And my lunatic's laugh.

<u>Cold Welding</u>

If you bring together
Two things alike,
Two metals,
Completely pure,
And put them under tremendous pressure,
They will fuse.
They form one single cohesive entity.
I'm not sure why this happens.
I'm not the right kind of scientist
To explain such a phenomenon.
I am,
However,
A person with eyes,
And ears,
And skin,
And a tongue.
I have a nose
For lived experiences.
I and I'll tell you this,
All for free;
Cold Welding feels frightfully familiar.
I've been under pressure before.
Crushing pressure.
The kind that holds your ribs tight
And squeezes the very heart of you.
That kind of pressure
Is destructive.
Terrible.
Inescapable.
"Pressure,"

Hymns For The Gallows Part Two

They say,
"Turns coal to diamonds."
I am not a diamond.
I never will be.
A diamond is beautiful,
Valuable,
Desirable,
But ultimately it's
Cold,
Hard,
And discrete;
Separate from all around it.
Diamonds are set in something,
Or the tip of something,
But never really part of it.
I have felt the pressure.
I feel it every single day,
Like a diver
Deep beneath the inky waves.
I have not become a diamond,
Because I am not some dusty,
Dirty,
Polluting lump of carbon.
I am a person.
A human being.
Flesh
And blood
And bone
And tooth
And hair
And nail
And soul.

Eleanor Fitzgerald

I have felt the pressure.
It almost crushed the life out of me,
But it didn't.
I encountered someone the same.
Someone pure.
And we bonded.
Fused.
Became one entity.
Together, we were stronger.
The pressure continued,
And we grew.
More and more and more
Pure souls flocked to us,
And we flew our flags.
We bonded.
In the terrible pressure of an intolerant society
We were cold welded together.
Now we're strong.
Now we're proud.

Bastard Man

There he goes,
The Bastard Man,
Doing his Bastard Crimes,
Thieving food,
Skulking shadow,
Watcher in the dark.
There he goes,
The Bastard Man,
Toward his Bastard Throne.
King of Camelot,
Out in the open,
Boldest of the trio.
Come hither to me,
Oh Bastard Man,
So I may show you love.
Scoundrel.
Ruffian.
Thief of my heart.
Welcome home,
Bastard Man,
To your chosen family.
Ragtag.
Strange.
Yours.
Forever.

Eleanor Fitzgerald

<u>Sparks</u>

Embers drift skyward,
Sparks in the night sky.
I rescued you from those flames,
My oldest friend.
My blue-eyed protector,
My fuzzy furred confidant.
You're as old as me,
As old as time when viewed through my eyes.
Inseparable.
Uneclipsed.
But one day I grew up.
I saw the past.
The flames.
The Horror.
Reflected in those unblinking blue eyes.
Suddenly our bond was shaken.
Eclipsed by the weight of history.
You were there.
You saw everything
And said nothing.
My confidant now complicit.
My protector now found wanting.
What else could I do?
You stood in the stand.
Your silence;
Defiance or acquiescence?
I put you on trial,
Weighed the history
Of all you've witnessed

Hymns For The Gallows Part Two

With the comfort you've given.
You, the dearly departed,
And I, Anubis.
Tears blurred my eyes
As I measured your leaden heart.
You're guilty, old friend,
And the sentence is death.
But a lifetime of friendship
Does not count for naught.
I commuted your sentence,
And kept you clutched to my chest.
Companion,
Confidant,
Traitor,
Criminal,
But I'd risk it the flames once again,
For you,
My oldest friend.

Eleanor Fitzgerald

Ill Met By Moonlight

You thought you were safe this time.
Of course,
You'd privately wondered about the monsters
Lurking within the hearts
Of all your dearest friends.
But not this one.
Certainly not tonight,
Of all nights.
You never expected this to happen,
But as you type your careful reply,
"I'm just not looking for a relationship right now",
A sliver of moonlight falls across your DMs.
The creature,
Your former friend,
Howls in anguish as the change takes him,
And from his human form,
The Nice Guy emerges.
His hands form claws,
Itching to type the words 'fucking bitch'.
The fur grows fast and thick
Around his tremulous throat.
No "Ahwooo!" escapes his lips;
Only cries of "Friendzoned again!"
In a fit of rage,
He claws from his head,
The fedora,
That he will petulantly declare is a trilby.
He is called,
Not to hunt,
But to the incel forums which haunt his daylight thoughts.

Hymns For The Gallows Part Two

You can't see this of course,
But judging from the vitriol spewing from his keyboard,
It's not a bad metaphor.
You sigh heavily,
Shaking your head,
As you step away from the computer.
You did not expect this,
Certainly not tonight,
Of all nights.
The curtain shifts at the open window,
Stirred by the summer breeze.
The light of the moon graces your face
As the message alerts come thick and fast.
You are not a bitch.
But as your teeth lengthen,
And your tail sprouts,
You acknowledge that 'She-Wolf',
Would be fairly accurate.
Your blood sings,
As the Gift envelops you.
Tonight,
Of all nights,
You feel so wonderfully alive.
As you scrape your claws
Down the metal frame of your bed,
Sharpening and sparking in equal measure,
You see his last message.
"Girls like you are never interested in nice guys like me!"
You leap through the open window
Into the moonlit night.
As the call of the hunt fills your heart,
You have one final thought,

Eleanor Fitzgerald

Accompanied by a wolfish grin.
Be careful what you wish for.

<u>There's Something About Flags, Part One</u>

"A time when Dinosaurs ruled the Earth!"
But did they really rule it?
Or were they simply just vibing?
After all,
There are no flags
In the Fossil Record.
Flags are a modern concept,
In the grand scheme of things.
A way of saying
This is me!
I live here!
And I love that for people,
Until it's shit.
They draw lines in the dirt.
This is mine!
I own here!
The question sticks in my throat,
"How can you claim this place?
People already live here!"
And you shake your head
In pity and contempt.
"They don't have a flag,"
You say,
"So they can't really be people."
Those people,
They carried their flag all over the world.
New flags were made
When people hated the old ones,
And those flags were carried
To lands that did not want them.

Eleanor Fitzgerald

All over this blue world,
Above it too.
"We came in peace,
For all mankind"
Written beneath the Flag,
So carefully planted.
The flag of the only nation
To use nuclear weapons in anger.
"I do it because I love you"
Says the abuser,
As they wipe the tears
From your bruised and bloodied face.
I hate those flags.
The ones on a soldier's uniform.
The Flag of a Nation.
They swear their lives to it.
End the lives of others,
Who do not want it in their land,
Replacing their flag.
I do not care for nations.
Nor armies.
Nor borders.
I despise those flags,
But not all flags.
Some flags,
I adore.
The ones that loudly proclaim
This is Me!
I am Alive.
Those flags,
Are flags to be proud of.
I have one of those flags,

Hymns For The Gallows Part Two

Pink, White, and Blue.
It's a signal,
A sign,
Semaphore to my siblings;
You are not alone.
After a Pride Parade,
The Woman asks
"Why do you have to have a flag?"
Because,
Mother,
It's the only language you understand.

Eleanor Fitzgerald

Blood Sugar

I'm a monster,
I'm a vampire,
A horror of the silver screen.
Blood sick and love-drunk,
I walk the city at night.
Bathed in moonlight,
Longing for the limelight,
I hate the way they look at me,
Yet I'm dying to be seen.
I'm the monster,
I'm the danger,
I'm the horror plastered across the tabloid rags.
Denied so many rights,
Shown little but wrongs,
The sweetness of my life fades.
My blood sugar plummets;
A transphobia driven hypo,
Don't bother waking me.
Because I'm a monster,
I'm the horror,
I'm the killer of my mother's son.
Up for discussion,
Always debated,
Tell me,
Do you have an opinion too?
Yes, Doctor, I'm the Monster,
Yes, Doctor, I'm the Horror,
Yes, Doctor,
I like to wear dresses too.

Hymns For The Gallows Part Two

Opened up,
Torn asunder,
In the gender clinician's chair.
Yes, Doctor,
I sometimes touch myself,
No, Doctor,
I hate my voice,
Of course, Doctor,
I'll say whatever you want me to.
I emerge as a monster,
As a horror,
As a transwoman in a transphobe's world.
"Tell me," says the woman with the cigarette,
"Did they make you hate yourself too?"

Eleanor Fitzgerald

<u>They Work You Hard</u>

It's hard work,
For less than a dollar a day.
My back hurts,
From shovelling all day.
The weight of it all;
The tremendous
Incomprehensible
Mountain of bullshit
That I have to shift.
My fingers hurt,
From pulling all the spikes.
Sharp and sudden
An intake of breath,
Sucking on my pricked digits,
All copper and tang.
Now is not the time for kid gloves,
Not gloves of any kind;
I must grip the barbs
And pull the thorns.
My feet hurt,
From all the standing.
Standing up for myself,
Standing my ground,
Standing on ceremony.
Although,
On my weary feet
There are things
That I will not stand for.
My throat hurts,
From all the choking

Hymns For The Gallows Part Two

Down your saccharin cruelty.
From swallowing
All the words
That I'm not supposed to say.
From suffocating
In the dust that covers
Your musty ass
Outdated opinions.
You take my breath away,
And now I have to buy it back.
My eyes hurt,
From all the tears I've shed
And the grave dirt flung
Into my face as I bury him,
And her,
And them,
And you,
And one day me.
I will have chance to rest my eyes
To grab forty winks
When I'm in the deep
And the dark.
My heart hurts,
From all the Emotional labour,
Without a union.
No paid time off,
Certainly not with
All the wheres
Whats
Whys
And Hows
That I have to answer

Eleanor Fitzgerald

All for free.
For less than a dollar a day,
It's hard fucking work.

Poison

I'm supposed to be nice to them. That's the real kicker, the bit that I just can't stomach or swallow; I have to be nice. Oh, sure I'm a pleasant enough person to all and sundry, but not to someone who's done me harm.

No, sir, that is a line in the fucking sand.

Sure, they don't realise the extent of what they've done; of what they're a part of, but that's only because they don't care to look. Sure, it'll break the camel's back but to the person placing it it's just another piece of straw. You can decry them for their part, of course, but they'll throw their hands up and beg ignorance; how could I know, how could I foresee such a thing?

As I've said, they didn't even care to look.

But here I am, getting ahead of myself again. That's the problem; I get so worked up that I lose the thread and yell about niceties. I get so wound up in metaphor that I can't see the wood for the, well, camels, in this case.

Let me take a breath.

Let us take a step back.

Begin at the beginning.

But first, a little word of warning, a public service announcement of sorts; you're not going to like this story. If you're transgender, you're going to recognise yourself in me, and it's going to make you angry. If you're not, you might realise that you're complicit, that you too have straw in your hands, and that's going to make you uncomfortable at best.

Good.

I want you to sit with that. Maybe you'll learn something important from it, maybe you'll just feel so shamefaced that you'll put the straw down; not because you think what you've done is wrong, mind, but because I'm looking at you while you do it.

Either way, that slightly uncomfortable sensation of eels squirming in the pit of your belly right now is exactly what I want you to feel. It means that you're listening, and not just waiting to speak.

Now that I have your ears, I'd like your eyes next.

I want you to picture me, all sallow skin and sunken eyes, all blackened gums and stringy hair, standing shakily before you. I don't think any more details are necessary; my appearance isn't anywhere near as important as the question that arises from it, the one on your lips.

What happened to you?

Well, my friend, I'm so glad that you asked.

I've been poisoned.

What a phrase; I've been poisoned. It implies such agency, and begs so many questions.

Who poisoned you?

What poisoned you?

Why were you poisoned?

Now, I'm sure you can make an educated guess given the 'us' and 'them' I laid out earlier, but let's make things explicit so nobody can feign ignorance.

Why? Because I'm transgender, obviously. I am different, defective; deviant, even. In the eyes of cisgender society I am the other and the monster. I am the vermin in a perfect world; a rat ripe for poisoning.

With what? Transphobia, of course. I am poisoned with hate, both casual and systemic; I will elaborate shortly.

We have the means and the motive; it's time to ask the final question.

Who did such a thing? Well, not to put too fine a point on it; you did. Oh, I know that you were not alone in such a terrible deed, but you didn't exactly try to stop it either. After all, straw laden hands doth camels' backs break.

Transphobia isn't poison!

Isn't it?

It certainly turns your blood icy in your veins. The slightest dose will hasten your heartbeat and chill your sweat. A mouthful sours your stomach and loosens your bowels to water, and it only worsens from there. Blurred vision, disorientation, and mental confusion; a sense of impending doom. Like a rat in a trap there is no way out; no respite or release in a cisnormative society.

But that's the point, isn't it?

The poisoner's ultimatum; you will go back or you will die.

Sure, plenty of us do carve out lives for ourselves in your world, but those are never the lives you shout about, are they? You only show those that detransition or perish and even then you don't give us dignity in death.

But, you say insistently, *transphobia is not poison!*

I disagree. Like poison, transphobia is something you are exposed to, one way or another, until you cease to function; it builds up in your heart and soul. You still can't see it though, can you?

Take a look through my eyes.

Come see the world you have made.

It starts, as things often do, in the media. There, in the cinema; the cross-dressing murderer slicing up swathes of beautiful women. On the television; the hideous man in the dress prancing about before the laughter track. In the comedy halls; the attack helicopters and snide comments delight the masses. On the computer; trans people exploited and degraded into a cisgender fetish. In the news broadcasts; evil endocrinologists prey upon children too young to know themselves. In the blog posts; concerns are raised about the epidemic of lost lesbians.

And in the newspapers; surely even you aren't so blind as to miss it here?

What does this background roar seek to create if not an air of hostility and toxicity?

It starts in the media, and the resulting miasma fills our lungs, choking and blinding us. I've long since forgotten what it was to breathe easily; pollution and suffocation are my normality.

With air as poisoned as this, it's no wonder there are so many obstacles to declaring oneself trans; heaven forbid we expose one of you to all of this by accident! Why, then you might actually decide to do something about it.

To protect you we are held up to a mercury mirror of everything you say we should be to become palatable to you; everything we are told we are not. This happens again and again, our noses held ever closer to the surface by our quicksilver questioners. I've never met anyone who enjoys those appointments.

Mercury drives you mad, don't you know.

And now, my friend, now we get to you.

Some of your poisoning is overt; explicitly lethal doses held high in glinting syringes. Rape, violence, exploitation; these are what you expect to see. And whilst these envenomed events are among the most spectacular that I have experienced, they are by far the least common.

The sideways glances, the shaking of the head, the disgusted frown; the sheer disappointment that I face from the public each and every day is the fallout I must endure for my choice to keep on living. The metallic taste on my tongue is a constant reminder that this is a world not made for me; this is a life that I'm not expected to survive.

And each and every bit of it is deliberate. In fact, it would be easier for you not to do this; I don't understand you. I am so very very angry, but I must take stock and save room for just a little more, for we have come full circle.

Hymns For The Gallows Part Two

I'm supposed to be nice to you.

Oh, sure, you'd forgive my anger at everyone I've mentioned up until now, but you've done nothing wrong, right?

Are you so fucking sure?

Have you ever told me how brave I am? Have you ever pointed out how hard it must be? Have you ever waved your arm at all the transphobic institutions and lamented at how awful my life will become?

Have you ever put the poison into my hands and expected me to eat it? Have you ever smiled a false smile or cried crocodile tears at the unbalanced life I'm supposed to be thankful for, even though your thumb is firmly on the fucking scales?

Have you ever done any of these things and expected me to say thank you? Your pity and contempt are not so cleverly hidden as you might think.

I can deal with being poisoned.

But forcing me to partake in my own destruction and expecting me to be grateful for it?

No, sir, that is the line in the fucking sand.

I hope you've been paying attention.

Let's check in, shall we?

How do those eels in your stomach feel now?

I've only got one last thing to say to you, my straw carrying friend, so listen up.

You, yes you, are a special kind of evil, and I hate you most of all.

But it's not literal poison!

No.

No, it isn't.

It's trauma, which is so much worse. Not all trauma is a bolt from the blue; in fact, much of it builds up so slowly that you don't notice until it's far, far too late.

At least with poison you can vomit it up, or take an antidote. Trauma has to be outgrown. Trauma has to be examined, understood, and extracted with time and therapy; this is difficult.

In fact, it's nearly impossible if one is constantly being traumatised.

Straw by straw.

Blow by blow.

Drip by drip.

Day by day.

And that's the problem with poison.

It accumulates.

This isn't a nice story; it's the tale of a murder.

Don't you dare try to apologise to me.

I'm already dead.

<u>Bone to Ash</u>

I was born with the smell of smoke
About my face.
Acrid,
Black and thick,
It permeated everything in my home.
The smell of smoke was comforting,
Ubiquitous,
Almost intimate in its closeness.
But I did not realise
There is a fire.
I didn't read the papers.
I wasn't one for the internet,
Not yet at least,
But I did go to the pictures.
I consumed cinematographic delights
Laced with with accelerant.
So when I did read the papers
The embers caught with frightening vigour.
It felt safe
In the warmth of the many,
But also uncomfortably hot,
Because
There is a Fire.
The flames first singed
The hairs on my manly arms,
And darkened my body with soot;
A five o'clock shadow at nine a.m.
But you still don't notice.
You think the smell
Is your Father's pipe smoke

Eleanor Fitzgerald

And you smile
As your Mother
Sings you into your grave.
I am not crazy.
There is a Fire.
We turn our eyes to heaven,
Praying for rain.
A little cold shower,
A brief downpour,
Some goddamn peace.
But God won't engage us,
At least that's what they say.
Although isn't it pretty,
The falling stars?
White Phosphorus Words,
Alight upon our hospitals.
They come for the children first,
Although it will soon be our turn.
The public applauds them,
Gives them prizes,
As they try to consult and reform us
Out of existence.
There is a Fire.
But they say it's for our own good.
They shake their heads,
And judge us for our burns,
For our bones made ash,
As though they aren't all arsonists,
As though they aren't all to blame.
Every "Fag" a cigarette butt,
Every "Tranny" an ember,
Every "Lost Lesbian" a flame.

Hymns For The Gallows Part Two

And they have the audacity to ask
Why we are so afraid!
THERE IS A FIRE.
And yet you're still here,
Still reading,
And listening,
To those who pour gasoline.

Eleanor Fitzgerald

Part Two: Piece de Resistance

Eleanor Fitzgerald

Piece de Resistance

The steak is rare and bloody; Dark smiles with every single bite. She chews slowly, savouring the warm, juicy morsel. Edgar is smiling too. He's patiently waiting for Dark to continue her story.

"So," Dark says at last, "I thought coming out would be the hard part, but that just wasn't the case."

"No?"

"Okay, well, it wasn't easy, that's for sure, but I only had to do it once for each person."

"I take it not everyone reacted that well."

"My mother certainly didn't, but most of my friends did. Well, I thought they did, anyway. After what Ariadne said..."

"You'll always have some friends that have knives behind their backs, but most will stand true. I've decades of experience, after all."

"The hardest part was all the little jabs and pokes. The way people spoke to me, they way they looked at me, the things the newscasters on TV said; hell, even an author I once loved and looked up to just couldn't help herself, it seems.

"So much hatred, so often, just grinds a person down, you know? It makes it hard to keep on going."

Dark puts down her cutlery as her lip quivers. Edgar walks over to her and places a comforting hand on her shoulder.

"Can I tell you a little secret?"

"Uhuh," Dark says, sniffling.

"I never write down any of the bad things, unless someone really wants me to. It's like a photograph, you know? We only ever take pictures of the good times because they're what keeps us going when all around is dark.

"So why don't you tell me about the good bits? The times and

36

events and people that made you laugh and smile and feel unashamedly yourself; why don't you tell me about those?"

Dark sits quietly for a few more minutes, eating several more mouthfuls of her sumptuous meal.

A thick rare porterhouse steak with a port and shallot jus, garlicky mashed potatoes, minty peas, and grilled mushrooms comprised the penultimate course of Dark's short life.

"I've never been wealthy, not once before or after my transition; this sort of thing," she says gesturing to her plate, "was the stuff of dreams for me."

"So, Dark, tell me about something that makes you smile."

She pauses for a moment, before nodding softly to herself.

"One thing that surprised me, I guess, was just how much my voice could change with practice. It took a lot of hard work, but I went from having quite a deep, almost gravelly voice, to the more feminine, husky one I have now."

"I also realised that I loved singing, more than anything."

Edgar smiles at Dark, who lowers her head shyly.

"Will you sing something for me?"

"Why sing now?"

"Because singing is hopeful, and even now a little hope is a beautiful thing. Because even if you don't know it, you're the most alive you've ever been."

Dark closes her eyes and smiles for a moment before she starts to sing. Edgar is a little shocked at her choice of song; *End of the World* by Skeeter Davis.

The slow and melancholy tune fills the space between them for a few minutes, and once Dark is finished singing Edgar smiles appreciatively.

"Thank you, Dark. That was lovely."

"Thank you for asking me to sing." She snuffles slightly and wipes away a stray tear. "I'm sorry, that song always makes me cry."

"Not all tears are an evil, Dark."

"So, whilst we're being maudlin, how about I tell you about the first dress I ever bought as a woman? Not the tatty old thing that I hid beneath my mattress, but the real first dress; the one that made me feel like I was on the right path."

"Please do."

She sits back in her chair, grinning a little.

"So, there was a department store in the city that was having a closing down sale, so there were a lot of otherwise expensive dresses going cheap. I went there with a friend for moral support; he was lovely but had no eye for fashion whatsoever.

"We're going through the sale rails, both of us in jeans and tees, desperately looking for something to fit across my shoulders; no easy task, even now. We're getting a lot of sideways glances, but we continue our search.

"Eventually my friend makes this triumphant noise and holds up this crimson form-fitting dress, with silver rhinestones on the neckline. It was not what I'd wear now, for sure, but back then that dress shone like a beacon in the dark."

"Did you buy it?"

"I decided to try it on first. I went up to the changing room attendant, who gave me a little tag and pointed me to the empty cubicle without so much as a word.

"I had no idea how to put on this dress; my practice one buttoned at the front. I eventually dragged it on over my head, and wriggled it into place. It was a very snug fit, but it was a dress and it was in my size."

"How did it look?"

"Truthfully?" Dark says with a little smile.

Edgar nods.

"It looked fucking horrendous!" Dark bursts out laughing.

"Good god, what an ugly fucking dress! But although I looked absolutely awful, all short back and sides and square shoulders in this clingy thing, I felt incredible.

"I couldn't help but smile. It felt so right, like the tumbler of a safe just dropping into place; the first piece of the puzzle. I strode out to my friend, and he gave it the ol' awkward thumbs up, which was good enough for me.

"I walked out of there with that dress in a white paper bag and I felt ten feet tall. I wore it to a party that evening, with shoddy makeup and cheap perfume, but I wore it as a woman, and that was enough for me!"

"You said that this was a maudlin story; it sounds pretty cheerful to me."

"Oh, it is, for the most part. It's also that as I walked into the party that evening, I saw the looks other people gave me. In that dress I found my true self, but I also found out just how other people would look at me.

"I still have that dress, even though I don't wear it any more. It's sentimental, you know?"

"I understand."

"Like I said, there have been a lot of those looks over the years. That evening, before the party, my friend took me to one side and asked me if I was sure about this.

"I knew that it would be difficult in the short run, but I hoped that it would get easier; that one day I would look back and smile."

"You're smiling now."

"It's bittersweet, Edgar. It's not the joyous grin I thought I would have."

"Some things just don't go as we expect them to." Edgar says softly.

"In the trial, I found myself looking back and wondering if my transition was worth all the trouble and pain it had caused me."

"Was it?"

"Yes. Yes, and it still is," Dark says softly. "I just thought I'd have more time, you know?"

"You want the truth, Dark?"

Dark pauses for a moment, before nodding.

"There's never enough time, no matter who you are."

Raindrops

"Excuse me, but could you tell me if it's raining, please?"

It's a simple enough question, but it seems to catch so many people out.

"I'm sorry, what?"

Yes, you heard me right the first time, but I'll repeat it just so you're sure.

"Outside; is it raining?"

Then, of course, the inevitable response.

"There's something strange about you."

That's what people have said to me my entire life. They say that I feel like I'm a little out of step with everyone else, a little out of place; they think that I don't belong. I can't say that I blame them, as I feel it too. I can never quite settle or relax, and people's eyes seem to slide off me, like they would rather look anywhere else.

People get agitated when I spend a long time around them; they rearrange furniture, shift repeatedly in their seat, or try to remember something that they're sure they've forgotten. It would almost be funny if it wasn't so isolating.

I know that I'm supposed to wonder and agonise forever about what is wrong with me, but in truth I actually know exactly why my life is like this. It all goes back to the seventh of April, back in nineteen ninety six.

We were at the beach, my parents and I, and I was splashing around in the surf. I was only little, just seven years old, and my life was tough but good. Sure, we didn't have a lot of money, and my parents worked hard to give me the best life they could. My dad had never been the same since his accident in ninety three, and my mum had to work especially hard to make up for it, but they loved me unconditionally and without restraint.

I'm sorry, I don't mean to get emotional.

41

I just miss them so very much.

Where was I? Oh, yes, the ocean. Ever since that day I've wondered what it is about water that makes it so special; I've spoken to theologians, physicists, and everyone in between. Always water, for some reason, and sometimes the things caught in it too. Flotsam and jetsam.

Yes, I know I'm stalling.

Talking about a traumatic event is never easy, especially when it changed your life as markedly as mine did. It's difficult; more so as you've got that look in your eyes, a kind of impatient doubt. Would it kill you to cut me a little slack?

I'm sorry, I shouldn't snap. I just want you to understand is all. I've never actually spoken to, well, anyone about this, let alone a crisis counsellor. It's a tremendously awkward experience after all, but hopefully not one I'll have to repeat. Lesson learned; it's down the road, not across the street.

No, please don't write that down.

It was a joke; I'm still stalling for time.

Right; April seventh, ninety six, that fateful beach. I'm not entirely sure what happened, but I lost my footing. I went right under the water and the current dragged me out, under the waves, faster than you can possibly imagine. I was rolled over and over; it was agony. As my breath finally gave out and the water entered my lungs, everything went strange for a moment.

The world felt out of alignment, off kilter.

And then it snapped back and I was dumped on the beach coughing and spluttering the water from my lungs. I heard raised voices and felt hands on me; my parents' hands. Only they weren't my parents, not really.

I was somewhere different. Sure, the beach was broadly the same but this was a much chillier day and the sand was a slightly different colour. Everything was just a little bit wrong.

Hymns For The Gallows Part Two

Except for my parents.

They were a lot wrong.

My mother's lined face and mop of short grey curls were now the platinum blonde locks of a much younger looking woman; one who'd had an easy life. Her eyes were the same piercing blue, but there was something hidden behind those eyes; I would discover the truth soon enough.

My father on the other hand... Well, he was seemingly a younger man too; certainly an unscathed one. He still had both of his arms, and there were no scars on his face. Whereas my dad, my real father, would've looked at me with love and concern, this man just looked at me with contempt.

I reached out for the woman, my mother, and my advances were met with a slap so hard that it set my ears ringing. That set the tone for the rest of my life.

Whilst my real parents weren't rich or successful, they weren't ever cruel to me. Hell, I don't even think they would comprehend the things that man and woman did to me. I had to endure that for eleven years; as soon as I was old enough, I left home.

I changed my name and I disappeared; you see, they insisted that I had a different name to the one I had been given by my real parents. I am Isaac, though, and I always have been.

I tried to tell anyone that would listen that I wasn't from this world; that I was trapped here by some cosmic accident. They all just looked at me like I was crazy, spoke to me like I was crazy, and made me see shrink after shrink.

You know, if enough people tell you that you're crazy, you'll start to believe it. I certainly did. I pushed down all the nonsense about a parallel life until I was nineteen years old. You can spend a lifetime trying to bury the truth, and something as innocuous as a rainy Friday afternoon can bring all the lies crashing down.

I was sitting in the window seat at the top of the stairs, just watching the rain trickle down the window. I was enjoying myself; I had a cup of tea in my hands and music in my ears. Then my housemate asked what I was doing.

"Watching the rain," I replied. I was lazily tracing the path of one particular raindrop down the pane. My housemate blinked, and then brought my world tumbling down.

"Isaac, mate, it's not raining."

Yet there I was, watching the rain pour. That's when it hit me; all my life, ever since that fateful day, I'd been seeing water that wasn't there. Puddles, rain, strange tides, and floodwaters; I'd comment on it, but nobody would listen. Why would they?

I was just a mad child.

But that afternoon I knew what I was seeing was real. I went outside into the rain and I felt the warm summer shower on my skin, yet I remained bone dry. I knew what this was; this was the rain that was falling back in my world.

Back home, where I belonged.

I won't bore you with all the investigations I undertook, with all the experiments I carried out; I threw so much time and money down that hole. What I will tell you, however, is just how many people go missing in water. Dozens every year in rivers, lakes, oceans, rainstorms, snow, and even bathtubs.

No discernible pattern. No repeatability. Nothing.

All the while, I'm left stranded in this world. I'm alone, isolated, and out of place. I am uncomfortable, both to others and within myself.

You have no idea how awful my life is.

How desperately alone I am.

I try to take heart in the fact that whoever it was that replaced me would've had a good life with my mum and dad; they would've escaped the monsters stuck in this world. I try to take heart in that, but I can't.

Hymns For The Gallows Part Two

Desperation wins out in the end; it always does.

Given that my first crossing was in a life or death situation, I decided to try to emulate the same conditions. I ran myself a nice warm bath, took some sleeping pills, and then tried to open my wrists. I still wonder if it would've worked if my housemate hadn't barged in and called the paramedics; I was doubtful, to be honest, but it would've been an end to my misery either way.

You have no idea what it's like to be seen as crazy by literally everyone in the world. I can see the disbelief in your eyes; your poker face is not as good as you think it is. What does it matter? You're just going to lock me up anyway.

Who knows, maybe I am crazy. Look out the window, at all the people in short sleeves and summer dresses; they don't see the rain pouring around them. They have no idea what it's like.

You have no idea what it's like.

Wait.

Really?

I... After all these years!

Please tell me that you aren't lying. Can you really see it too?

Placeholder for a Confession

I was going to write something pithy.
Something snide.
I was going to write about alcohol,
And how much I want a drink
As soon as I wake up in the morning.
But I was going to trivialise it.
Make it quirky.
Fun, even.
But it isn't fun,
Is it?
My partner's liquor collection
Sits on a shelf across the room.
Five steps,
A twist of a bottle cap,
And I'm free.
It's Burns Night next week,
And my colleagues suggested online drinks.
I agreed.
The first week is a little early,
In my opinion,
To have the addiction talk.
So I'll attend,
Have a little whiskey,
And pass the rest off to someone else.
Someone who isn't me.
I was going to write about being an addict,
Which is true,
But also about being an alcoholic,
Which isn't.
I'm not an alcoholic.

Hymns For The Gallows Part Two

Alcohol doesn't have a hold on me,
And I can say no to a drink.
In fact,
I can't remember the last drink I had.
What alcohol is to me,
What alcohol does to me,
For me,
Even,
Is provide a placeholder for my true desire.
I don't want to be alive.
I haven't wanted to for the longest time.
I first tried to kill myself
Six thousand seven hundred and fifty seven days ago.
That's over eighteen years,
And I'm keeping count.
I think about ending my life
Every
Single
Day.
I'd be terrified if I didn't.
And,
Here comes the confession,
I still intend to.
Not today.
Not tomorrow either.
But one day.
I honestly can't see my life closing out any other way.
For a while,
I tried to outlast it.
Just get through today,
I told myself,
And tomorrow will be better.

But tomorrow was just another today.
And tomorrow
And tomorrow
And tomorrow
Until I couldn't walk unaided.
Until I looked older than I ever thought I would.
Until instead of friends
All I have is a lengthening list of names
That hurts every time I read it.
Until I'm alone.
I lay awake every night.
I can't stop thinking
About stopping all thought
Forever.
It's strange.
This poem has gone on a lot longer
Than I ever intended.
It keeps going
And going
And going
Like a lifeline,
Deepening on an ageing palm.
A darkening lifeline,
In contrast to hesitation marks
That scar my wrists,
Shining brighter
Than any future I can envision for myself.
And yet,
I made the poem longer again.
We all have to stop somewhere though,
So raise a glass
As I cut it short.

<u>There's Something About Flags, Part Two</u>

Maybe,
Just maybe,
I'm colourblind.
Were the fluttering flags
Actually red instead of green?
This has happened all throughout my life.
Maybe,
Just maybe,
I'm a rag-crazed bull,
A red flag fluttered by a matador,
Sends me charging towards my doom.
What a cruel sport.
Maybe,
Just maybe,
I've been in England far too long.
Streets lined with bunting;
The signifier of a party,
A celebration,
A jubilee.
But,
Maybe,
Just maybe,
I don't know any other kind of love.

China Clay

I only lived in a mining village
For one month.
A wet and grey December.
It started drizzling the day I arrived
And it never let up,
At least not until I crossed the river.
You know which one I mean.
The river.
Whilst the tin mines
Lie dormant and crumbling,
The China Clay Machine
Roars with preternatural life.
It tears and scars the land,
Leaving mountains in its wake,
The Cornish Alps,
That's what they call them.
The fresh clay-stained soil
Provides a cast-off snow cap.
In that December
I walked those peaks
And beheld the gaping pits,
Grey and bleak as the leaden sky above.
The alkaline pools
That gathered in those man-made valleys
Were the deepest blue I'd ever seen.
Azure.
Sapphire.
Sparkling jewels in so much devastation.
I only lived there for a month,

But the clay will always stay with me.
The dust hung in the air.
It came down in the rain and coated everything.
I could never get clean.
The whole place felt so grey,
So bleak,
So depressing.
The dust gets into your lungs.
The greyness gets into your soul.
The mine waste,
The slag,
The detritus,
Is made into uncertain bricks,
For unstable housing,
For dispensable miners.
I lived in a mining village once,
Some years ago,
For a grey, wet December.
Under skies coloured and polluted,
By China Clay.

Eleanor Fitzgerald

Thirteen Dimensional Hyperplane

Can you see it?
Visualise it?
Imagine it?
A thirteen dimensional hyperplane?
No?
Me neither,
And I've listened to a lot of Prog Rock in my time.
I've taken a shitload of drugs too,
And I just can't see it.
That's fine though
Because
Sometimes
Some things
Are beyond our own perception.
Beyond our own experiences.
My post-transition life,
For example,
Looked the same to pre-transition me,
As a thirteen dimensional hyperplane.
Unimaginable.
Unknowable.
Impossible.
Oh, sure,
It was theoretically achievable,
On paper.
I mean,
The mathematics said it *should* be possible,
But it wasn't,
Not at that point at least.
It was unrealistic.

Hymns For The Gallows Part Two

Until I took that leap.
Until I passed beyond the pale.
Until I abandoned the realistic
For the sublime.
Sure, I'm a scientist,
But I also believe in magic.
Each time I see the woman in the mirror,
I think to myself,
How could I not?
I have abandoned the shallow
Two dimensional life
That I used to haunt.
I have discerned the transmundane
And am adrift in the mathematics.
I am dancing upon
The thirteen dimensional hyperplane
To the heartbeat of the universe
And it's like light;
Fantastic!

Horny Peppers and Bathtub Nudes

I adore my body.
The softness of my tummy,
The fullness of my breasts,
The strength of my arms,
The infectious glow of my smile,
The curl of my hair,
And the curve of my silhouette,
Are all beautiful.
I feel desirable.
I didn't always
However.
My view of my flesh
Was dry
Stark
Flat
Uninspiring
Unenthused.
I didn't ever think I'd see myself
In the way that I saw others.
But then,
One day,
My eyes were opened,
By my sister,
Of all people.
She is,
Among other things,
A photographer,
And a disciple
Of Edward Weston.
He was a photographer

Hymns For The Gallows Part Two

In the 20's and 30's,
Who understood desire.
His nudes of women,
Were deliberately stark,
Technically brilliant,
But profoundly clinical.
His peppers,
However,
Ugh.
I have never wanted
To fuck a vegetable before.
His peppers were oiled,
Shadowy,
Curvaceous,
Profoundly erotic.
I wanted to run my tongue over those peppers,
Slip my fingers into those dimples and crevasses.
Hold it up to my lips and just-
Whew!
I got a little carried away there.
But it changed the way I looked at myself,
Forever.
I want to be consumed.
I want you to adore my body.
I want you to see me,
To witness my sensuality,
But at a distance.
Today I am still too fragile to touch,
So I'll send you a picture instead.
All blossoms and breasts,
Nipples and naughty smiles,
Naked in the bathtub.

Eleanor Fitzgerald

You can't tell how soft I am
How good I feel,
So I'll show you.
Fingers digging into wet flesh,
Shine and shade,
In the most decadent waters
Of my life.
Epsom salt,
Rose Oil,
Rose Petals,
And two litres of creamy milk.
In that bath
All my shame is washed away.
I embrace my inner pepper,
Take some saucy,
Salacious pictures
That I'll share with all
Who want them.
To be wanted is deeply erotic.
What follows
After my handsy photo shoot,
In the bathtub,
After the click of the shutter,
Is mine to see alone,
But
You still have your imagination.

Nosegay

This city is in the grip of fear.
I can see it in the worried eyes
Of those who pass me
On stark and emptied streets.
I can hear it in the trembling voices
As I walk
Just a little too close.
But most of all
I can smell it.
It's on the air,
In my clothes,
And clinging to my nose.
Sharp.
Acrid.
Almost metallic,
Just a hint of ozone.
All that's missing is the crackle spark
Of the mad scientist's laboratory.
The stink of fear
Blinds me.
For in this city,
I can no longer find you.
I can track your subtle scent
Drifting on the summer breeze,
And follow it through street and junction
Until I am mere steps behind you.
But now,
Now,
You're one fearful smell in over a hundred thousand.
I can no longer saunter in your footsteps,

Eleanor Fitzgerald

Drinking you in.
I know you,
You see.
In fact,
I'd go as far as to say I know everything about you.
I know that sadness tinges your natural musk
On October eleventh,
Year after year.
I know that you have a preference for sweet popcorn,
Black licorice,
And granny smith apples.
I know what you wash your clothes in.
I know that you only wear perfume when you're nervous.
I know that you love to cook with ginger.
I know that you smell different when you're awake.
I know everything about.
Everywhere you've been
And everything you've done.
Your life is written clearly before me;
A novel in scent.
But I don't know your name.
We've never spoken,
Although so many times you've been close enough to touch.
But I have always refrained;
I wouldn't want to sully
Your delicate balance
With my own dreadful smells.
So, I have stood back
And enjoyed you from a distance.
But now I am drowning
In a sea of terror,
And you are nowhere to be found.

Hymns For The Gallows Part Two

This city is afraid,
And I fear along with them.
I have never felt so alone.

Eleanor Fitzgerald

<u>Bloodlust</u>

I came into being in this world,
Accompanied by blood and screaming.
The screams were not my mother's,
And nor was it the blood
Of the birthing bed.
The screaming was my own;
The tremulous wail
Of a true awakening,
Both primal and sexual.
The blood belonged to the one who showed me,
Who turned me,
Who brought me to life.
"You don't belong here"
She tells me.
"You don't fit this world,
And you don't know why."
We stood close to each other,
Her mouth by my ear,
Her words barely audible above the pounding bass.
I've never seen anyone so beautiful.
"This world of lights and noise
Has nothing for you,
Especially since they drove away
The blessed darkness
And hallowed silence.
It's too much for you,
Isn't it?"
She tugs gently on the hospital bracelet still on my wrist,
As her teeth find my throat.
The pain is overwhelming,

Hymns For The Gallows Part Two

Deep and sharp
But I begin to fade around the edges.
I'm slipping beneath the surface
And passing through the veil,
When my head rests gently in the hollow of her neck.
I don't know what drives me to bite her,
But as I drink deep
I feel alive in a way that I have never before.
My skin crackles with static
As the colour rushes back into the world.
My body twists and jerks
As she holds me close.
The change ravages my body,
Softening my skin,
And sharpening my teeth.
A fire starts in the pit of my stomach
Growing hotter
Denser
As it melts down through the core of me.
It settles in my loins,
Familiar and strange all at the same time.
As my thighs tighten
It burns brighter.
Explosive.
Fissile.
Unstoppable.
She holds me as I scream
And thrash
And give myself over to this feeling,
This thing that I have become.
Then the light fades,
And the tears come hot and fast

Eleanor Fitzgerald

As I realise that was the last sunrise
I'll ever experience.
She strokes my hair
As my I cry into her shoulder.
I see myself as she sees me;
A newly born vampire,
Weeping for the the innocence
I'll never reclaim.
Nothing will ever feel so intimate ever again.

Hymns For The Gallows Part Two

Poisoned Desire

I have a sweet tooth,
My love,
And not just in regards to the food I eat.
I crave the forbidden sugar
In all aspects of my life.
And you're a sweetheart,
My darling,
That much is true.
The rosy tint of your cheek
Is more enticing than the shining skin
Of any poisoned apple.
The sugar beaded sweat that trickles down your graceful, tender
neck
Is far sweeter than the nectar
Of any deadly flower.
The darkness that tinges your smile, deep and glittering,
Is more enthralling that the starry sky
Of any moonless night.
The strength of your pulse pulls me along
More forcefully than the beat
Of any piper's melody.
The intimate laughter that we both share
Drags me to my doom more irresistibly than the undulations
Of any siren's song.
You're a sweetheart,
My darling,
But that's not all.
There's a hint of threat within those Belladonna lips,
Jewelled eyes that call dart frogs to mind,

Eleanor Fitzgerald

Twinkle and shine.
Your skin is so pale, like white lead,
And just as temptingly sweet.
Nails all done up in orange and black;
There's something more fatal than faithful about this rosary
pattern.
There's a hint of dusky purple about yours eyes,
Nightshade dark and Foxglove bright.
Wormwood is shining high tonight,
Because you're a sweetheart,
My darling,
And a spoonful of sugar,
Helps the poison go down.

The Penrithen Song

I am currently writing a pulpy horror novel about the strange (and fictional) mining town of Penrithen. I wrote a shanty for the novel, and I wanted to share it with you here. If you feel like singing it, please find a rhythm to suit you.

We break our backs in the dark,
Beneath the rock and mud,
Every penny earned
Is bought with sweat and blood.
We go to work down in the mine,
Past the lifts and cables.
We shovel up the tin,
Until our bodies aren't able.

So, down we go!
Deep down below!
Kiss your love goodbye,
We're off to mine the tin
Beneath the rocky sky.
Down we go!
Deep down below!
Boys, kiss your girl farewell,
We're off to earn our money
In the pits of hell.

We often wish we were at sea,
Living life as sailors,
Or butchers, farmers, game keepers,
Bank tellers, and tailors.
And though we swear and grumble,

Eleanor Fitzgerald

About our aches and pains,
The dark is set into our souls,
And the tin flows through our veins.

So, down we go!
Deep down below!
Kiss your love goodbye,
We're off to mine the tin
Beneath the rocky sky.
Down we go!
Deep down below!
Boys, kiss your girl farewell,
We're off to earn our money
In the pits of hell.

The work is hard and the wage low,
We long for greater pay,
The Smugglers pay us shiny coin,
If we look the other way.
We wish to lie and rest in bed,
Before we grow too old.
Miners will wreck ships,
For the love of gold.

So, down we go!
Deep down below!
Kiss your love goodbye,
We're off to mine the tin
Beneath the rocky sky.
Down we go!
Deep down below!
Boys, kiss your girl farewell,

Hymns For The Gallows Part Two

We're off to earn our money
In the pits of hell.

Even in a miner's death,
No escape is found.
They'll nail you in a wooden box,
And you'll head back underground.
God cannot hear our prayers,
As we dig the tin and lead.
We're all now in the Devil's house,
So we pray to him instead.

So, down we go!
Deep down below!
Kiss your love goodbye,
We're off to mine the tin
Beneath the rocky sky.
Down we go!
Deep down below!
Boys, kiss your girl farewell,
We're off to earn our money
In the pits of hell.
Oh yes, my boys,
You kiss your girl farewell,
We're off to earn our money
In the pits of hell.

Eleanor Fitzgerald

Filet of Soul

I wish I knew you
In life, my dearest,
So you could have told me
Of your soul.
Instead,
You grace my table
And all that's left
Of you is a body.
But flesh,
My unknowing lover,
Is made of condensed soul.
So, please,
My dearest darling,
Let me taste your very being,
One morsel at a time.
Let me take my blade
And cut you,
So I may feel the warmth you keep inside.
I'll take a piece of lung,
For you leave me breathless.
Soft and yielding,
Like your voice.
Full, yet delicate,
Like your laugh.
A savoury taste
Of one I so desire to savour.
Next, a slice of liver,
For you make me feel so alive.
Tangy and sharp,
Like your wit.

Hymns For The Gallows Part Two

Warm and delectable,
Like your smile.
You are an acquired taste,
And I'm so glad I've acquired you.
Finally, a sliver of heart,
Seeing as you've taken mine.
Powerful, yet feather light,
Like your innocence.
Torn and bloody,
Like your final moments.
I'll consume you raw, my dear,
For you're the rarest taste of all.
Now,
As the after-taste lingers,
My butchered darling,
Let me bandage you
With my embalmer's hands.
As the flavour of your love persists,
My devoured dearest,
Let me smile for you
With my gore stained mouth.
As your body grows cold,
Oh, my sanguine lover,
Let me kiss you
With these blood drenched lips.
And in our final moments,
My departed Canopic Baby,
At last let me love you,
Like an Egyptian God of old.

Eleanor Fitzgerald

Part Three: Dessert

<u>Dessert</u>

"So," Dark says through a mouthful of pistachio ice cream, "I think one of the silver linings of this whole sorry affair is that it'll backfire on them."

"How do you mean?" asks Edgar.

"Well, I think the whole thing was a show trial. The Prosecution was an absolute hatchet job, after all, and my Defence was a shambles that didn't even plead the most obvious fact of my case!"

"Quite. You certainly are still alive and well."

"Yes," Dark says with a sigh. "For now, at least."

"Live in the moment, Dark."

"I am, Edgar, I am. Anyway, what was I saying?"

"A show trial and it backfiring."

"Ah, yes." Another pause for a bite of rich chocolate torte. "I know these people. I know how they think, and they thought they could railroad through a guilty verdict with that mockery of a court case, and string up someone like me.

"And to that end, they've succeeded, true. However, I don't think they're prepared for what's going to happen next."

"Which is?" Edgar has a small smile on his face and a twinkle in his eye.

"They think, wrongly, that it's going to scare us. They think that they'll terrify us back into the closet with the threat of the noose. And whilst initially people may be scared, they'll soon get angry.

"That's what they won't see coming; the backlash, the uprising. It won't be peaceful or polite. The time for niceness is over; the time for a bloody fight for the freedom of all transgender people is at hand."

"Do you really think that will happen if they hang you?"

"I can't say for certain, but I hope so. At least then all this mess will have been for a good cause. At least my life will have amounted to something, I guess."

"You're worth more than just your death, Dark." Edgar insists. "There are people in this world whose lives you've changed for the better, and they think about you all the time."

There's silence for a heartbeat or two.

"You really think so?" asks Dark quietly.

"I guarantee it."

"Well, my mother didn't seem to think so. She always used to hound me about how little I was doing with my life. Hell, even as a small child she used to tell me that I'd never amount to anything.

"That's not a thing a child needs to hear, you know? I wish, just once, that she'd told me I was enough; that she was proud of me."

"Well, I may not be your mother, but I certainly feel like I know you, Dark, and I'd be so proud to have a daughter even half as brave and kind and erudite as you."

"You really mean that?"

"I do." Edgar smiles across the dim cell. "There's more to family than just flesh and blood, Dark. Family is also the friends you surround yourself with and the community you build. I understand you more than you realise."

"Is that so?" Dark asks.

"Yes, it is."

"You've heard my story; I feel like I've talked all night. Do you feel like sharing?"

Edgar looks around conspiratorially before lowering his voice to just above a whisper. Dark leans in to listen.

"My mother died in childbirth, so I was raised by my father. He wasn't a bad man, but deep down I knew I was not the child he expected and that, even if he didn't mean to, he sometimes blamed me for my mother's passing.

"He was always good to me, although he often struggled to express his feelings towards me. He was a man from a much earlier time, you see, and he'd always taken my mother's lead in matters of the heart.

"I can only imagine what it must've been like, just after my birth. The love of his life cold in the ground whilst he was alone and adrift, with a baby girl he had no idea how to raise."

Dark sits up with a jolt.

"Wait, are you saying that you're tr-"

Her words are cut short as the cell door clangs open. Two men in black uniforms walk into the room with shackles in their hands. Their faces are expressionless, as are their voices as they speak.

"Dark Rose, your execution has been brought forward."

"Now?" Dark asks softly.

"Yes. Please come with us; it's time to go."

"Wait, it isn't dawn yet!" Edgar cries. "It's too early, too soon! This isn't how it's supposed to go!"

"It's alright, Edgar," Dark says softly. A sad smile plays about her lips. "I understand what you meant earlier, now."

She stands up from the table, straightening out her clothes. She places a hand on Edgar's shoulder and squeezes him softly.

"I'm ready."

A Grilled Cheese Sandwich at 3:27am

The gas catches light with a muted *whoomp*!
I snatch my hand away from the heat,
Quick and confident.
Even when I'm lost to the world around me,
I am found in the kitchen.
The butter in the pan hisses as it melts
As the knives snicker-snack.
My kitchen is alive with sound and I,
Unbidden,
Come to life with it.
Whenever I want to impress someone
I cook.
It's the one thing that I'm truly good at,
Or,
At least,
That I'll admit that I'm good at.
I never *want* to cook until I take that first plunge.
Afterwards,
However,
I cannot be stopped.
I am a woman possessed.
If I want you to fall in love with me
I'll cook for you.
Now,
As I stand here in the darkness both literal and figurative,
I cook.
I have chosen to turn my knives on my supper instead of myself.
I turn my appetite for destruction into gluttony for creation.
It's finished.

Eleanor Fitzgerald

I pause.
Take a bite.
Chew slowly.
If I want someone to fall in love with me,
I'll cook for them.
Tonight I love myself enough to keep on going.

Eleanor, Nicely

Now, be nice,
Eleanor,
My darling, my love.
They don't mean it.
It's not out of malice
Nor cruelty
Nor spite.
They just don't know any better,
Even though you've told them a hundred times or more.
You wear your badges so they can't forget.
Obvious,
Overt,
In their faces, even.
But still they misgender.
But still the deadname.
No matter how nicely I act,
I am still a tranny.
No matter how politely I speak,
I am still a shemale.
No matter how openly I exist,
I am still a trap.
I'm beginning to think that this might be deliberate.
But still they demand civility,
Niceties,
Pleasant small talk,
A deferential bow,
A demure hand.
Eleanor,
My darling, my love,

Eleanor Fitzgerald

Why are you shaking?
It is not cold; why do you tremble?
Your hands are empty; why do you clench your fists so tight?
You just need to be patient.
Polite.
Nice.
And one day,
Eventually,
Maybe,
They'll give you some rights.
Take heart, my darling,
Just do as they say,
And put down the gun.

Aurora

I've never seen
Those lights in the sky;
The fire of the Gods
High above me.
Now there's a chill in my spine
And static in the air;
You can tell that there's
Something coming.
I still remember your face
In the soft firelight
When we camped
In the northern starkness.
It's been oh so long
That I've been without you,
Since that night
The world went to darkness.
Green, amber, and gold,
Lit up the night sky.
You could hear it
Hiss and crackle.
One by one,
The systems all failed.
From the modern age
We all were unshackled.
I still remember your face
In the soft firelight
When we camped
In the northern starkness.
It's been oh so long
That I've been without you,

Eleanor Fitzgerald

Since that night
The world went to darkness.
In the beginning
We all came together.
My heart soared
When we didn't riot.
Then the nights got dark,
And folks went away
Just when did
The world get so quiet?
I still remember your face
In the soft firelight
When we camped
In the northern starkness.
It's been oh so long
That I've been without you,
Since that night
The world went to darkness.
I've been alone now
For all of twenty six years,
I've got good at lonely,
That much is true.
But every time I fall asleep
Under the roaring sky,
I just can't help
But miss you.
I still remember your face
In the soft firelight
When we camped
In the northern starkness.
It's been oh so long
That I've been without you,

Hymns For The Gallows Part Two

Since that night
The world went to darkness.

Eleanor Fitzgerald

The Uninvited

I think I need new glasses,
Or a new mirror
At the very least.
Clearly,
You must see
A different version of me
Than I see
Every
Single
Day.
My body must be contorted
A question mark
Made flesh.
Perhaps there's something
Written on my forehead,
Inviting your questions,
Comments,
Suggestions.
Your starter for ten,
Eleanor,
"Why can't you just be gay?"
Well,
My dear street random,
All I can say
Is that I've never been gayer.
Next up,
The comments section,
Like a flurry of post-its,
A cascade of bug logs;

It's fucking incessant.
"Real women don't dress like that."
"Why all the pronouns, just be a person?"
"Your gender is in your chromosomes."
Oh?
Is it really?
I hold up the delicate
Glass
Teardrop pendant
That contains my own wispy strands.
The very building blocks of me.
I hold myself up to the light,
Peer closely at my own ephemeral form.
Are you sure?
Because I can't see shit.
Although,
Maybe I do need new glasses.
It's noisy, though,
All these words.
They swarm about me like a flock
Of extremely belligerent pigeons.
I place my finger to my lips,
Asking for quiet,
I move it from mine to yours.
Ssssssssshhhhhhhhhhhhut the fuck up.
Of course,
The unasked question
Is the loudest,
Isn't it?
No.
No it's not.
I can tell you from experience,

Eleanor Fitzgerald

Because they will fucking yell it over the music
Playing on my headphones.
"Are you a boy or a girl?"
"Don't you care how you mother feels?"
"Did you cut your dick off yet?"
Why?
Are you tryna smash?
Cause I prefer my
Meaningful Overnight Relationships
To be a little more
Trans Positive.
By the way,
I've got a question of my own;
I'm sorry, but who the fuck are you?

Orbitoclast

I have a recurring dream
Where I am two different people.
The first is Eleanor the patient,
The mad woman strapped into a chair.
The second is Eleanor the doctor,
The cold woman with her tools to hand.
We talk, us Eleanors,
Without speaking or moving lips.
It's a dialogue of the soul.
Hegel would be so proud.
"You're broken, Eleanor."
"No, I'm not! I'm just different!"
"Different is defective in the eyes of the everyman, Eleanor."
"I don't care about them!"
"They care about you; they care because you need to fit in."
"Why? Why can't I just be left alone?"
"Just because, dear Eleanor. Please remember one thing, my
love."
"What?"
"Everything I do, I do because I love you."
The orbitoclast catches the light,
All silver and shine,
But somehow still shifting darkly.
The point gleams,
Trembles,
As it approaches Eleanor's eye.
Her pupils widen in fear,
In thrilled anticipation,
In clinical excitation.
Closer.

Eleanor Fitzgerald

Closer.
Closer still.
And then a moment of sharp pain and awful violation
As it pushes through.
The orbitoclast settles
As a gloved hand steadies,
Preparing for the first hammer blow.
The strike lands and the metal rings,
Resonating through Eleanor's skull.
Again
And again,
And again,
Ringing louder and more beautifully each time.
As the sound reaches a crescendo
The crack comes.
The breach.
The release.
The unmaking of a person.
I tense against the straps,
Then fall back as I look down at myself proudly.
I admire my handiwork.
A calm beauty.
Placid.
Ordinary.
An empty person.
"There you are, Eleanor dear,"
I say to my destroyed self.
"Now you're just like everybody else."

<u>Whales</u>

I have a grim fascination with whaling.
Not the modern kind,
All throbbing engines and polymer nets.
No,
My whalers were aboard sailing ships,
Mizzens fluttering in the breeze.
They had only their own two hands,
A few crude harpoons
And a flimsy row-boat,
To slay those titans of the deep.
Do I feel sorry for the whales?
Of course I do!
I'm not a monster.
But I'm less interested in the creatures being slain,
Than the minds behind the slaughter.
What sort of person looks at something so peaceful,
So beautiful,
So pure,
And decides to kill it?
Why, the industrious man, of course.
He sees valuable oil,
Bone for corsets and jewellery,
Priceless ambergris,
And not to mention the thrill of the hunt.
I often dream of being a whaler,
Barefoot in my boat,
Harpoon in hand.
I revel in the danger,
The exhilaration of a life and death struggle.
I always win, however.

Eleanor Fitzgerald

The water always darkens.
The thrashing always stops.
I am a strong man,
I am a rich man,
I am the whaler.
Only cheers come now;
The tears will flow later.
In the dark,
In my bunk,
I weep for the whales.
I weep for my darkening soul,
Because I know that tomorrow I will wake,
Pick up my harpoon
And kill again.

<u>Mortal Aeronauts</u>

Tell me,
Why do we dream of flying?
In the beginning,
There was The Fall.
Not necessarily from grace,
But
Something close enough
That the difference doesn't count.
Why do we dream of flying?
Why does our blood rush
As the turbine squeals at take-off?
I wonder how it felt,
To be in that cockpit
For that maiden flight.
The cough of the choke,
The thrum and roar of the propellers,
The wind,
Not only in hair,
But alive in the blood.
Like lightning.
Why do we dream of flying?
The static of our sleeping brains
Replays that first Fall
Over and over,
Jolting us awake.
The force of the Earth,
As we slip her crippling embrace,
Pulling on our organs
Is just another adrenaline spike.
Why do we dream of flying?

Eleanor Fitzgerald

We fight our wars in the air,
We rain death from up above,
Divine judgement
From Mortal Aeronauts.
No heavenly host
Could outfly or outfight
Mankind's technological marvels.
Why do we dream of flying?
Yet bury our dead?
What a cruel fate,
To dream forever
Of the open air,
Only to be interred
Beneath six feet of earth.
Trapped as wishful wings
Slowly fade to dust.
Why do we dream of flying?
We long to soar
For we were once angels.
Now we take to the air
With our mechanical flight,
And spit in the eye of God;
The one who clipped our wings
And put us on this earth.

Plague Doctor

Doctor, Doctor,
Gimme the news.
I feelin' trans,
And they say I'm confused.
Doctor, Doctor,
Is it true what they say?
That I've been forced
To be this way?
Doctor, Doctor,
Is it outta control?
Will bein' trans
Make me lose my soul?
Doctor, Doctor,
I can't help but ask;
Is it catching?
Why do you wear that mask?
Doctor, Doctor,
Are you sure you're right?
Because I'm livin' life
And I feel alright!
Doctor, Doctor,
My friends say it's grand,
How I smile,
When I say "I'm trans"!
Doctor, Doctor,
How 'bout you gimme some E?
'Cause I'm an adult,
And it's my body!
Doctor, Doctor,
Why so uptight?

Eleanor Fitzgerald

Self-determination
Is my right!
Doctor, Doctor,
Why all the strife?
Fuck the bigots,
Imma live my life!
Doctor, Doctor,
I know they lied!
I'm walking tall,
With bounce in my stride.
Doctor, Doctor,
I'm not the same!
I got a pair of Jimmy Choos
And a brand new name!
Doctor, Doctor,
Listen when I sing,
'Cause bein' trans,
Is a wonderful thing!

<u>Hyenas After Dark</u>

The giggle in the darkness,
Is different from the light.
You don't know what's coming;
The Hyenas are out tonight.
Up in your Ivory Tower,
You're having fun,
But when the chips are down,
Where will you run?
You've stolen our value,
And worked us to death,
We're scavengers now,
The Hyenas have nothing left.
Up in your Ivory Tower,
You're still number one,
But when the chips are down,
The poor will buy guns.
We're stalking the streets,
As blackouts sweep the land,
Hunger in our bellies,
And hatchets in hand.
Up in your Ivory Tower,
The mob's outside your front door,
You're trying not to listen;
Do you know what's in store?
You're a fat little piggy,
All you've done is feast.
The Hyenas are hungry,
Their laughs filled with teeth.
Up in your Ivory Tower,

Eleanor Fitzgerald

Only laughter through the phone,
The police are all eaten,
You must face us alone.
We break down the door,
We rush into the room,
All hoodies and hunger,
You're pulled to your doom.
Dragged from your Ivory Tower,
Screaming into the square.
You look around for pity,
But you'll find none there.
We raise up our hatchets,
The edges catch the light,
As the wet-work is finished,
The Hyenas feast tonight.
As the Tower burns in the distance,
The smoke thick and black,
The Hyenas together,
The Commune; the Pack.

Blood and Ink

This story is dedicated to Nicola Courtier; an old friend of mine. The first version of this tale was written as a gift for her some years ago now. It is with her blessing that I share this rewritten version with you.

Effie Beauclaire turned the heavy envelope over and over in her hands as the courier drove away from her small farmhouse cottage, his van bouncing along the rutted lane. She took the envelope in her teeth and picked up the small wooden chest that had been delivered at the same time.

Once the chest was upon the table, she made a cup of coffee and sat before the strange gift that had been given to her. The courier had said there would be a key inside the envelope, along with a letter explaining everything. He'd been unusually nervous, and had kept at an arm's length the entire time.

In one brief swipe of a well manicured nail, Effie opened the envelope. She tipped out an ornate brass key before extracting the letter. It was printed in dark green ink on rich, expensive paper. It was from a Solicitor's Office; Frères Rossignol, in Paris. Effie's brow furrowed. Why would a high-powered solicitor reach out to her, especially as she was all the way in Arbois?

Her bent brow was soon joined by a confused frown as she read the letter.

Dear Mme. Beauclaire,
I hope this letter finds you well. I do apologise for the intrusion into your life, but the items accompanying this missive have been held in trust by our firm for over two hundred years, and they were scheduled to be delivered into your possession.

95

For both the confidentiality of our clients and your own safety, if you are not Mme. Ephedra Beauclaire, please immediately stop reading this letter and telephone the number at the top of the page. Thank you for your cooperation in this matter.

Now, Mme. Beauclaire, the contents of the chest are twofold. Firstly, there are several articles that have been held in trust since the passing of one Nathalie Beauclaire in 1788; these are your inheritance as Nathalie Beauclaire is a distant relative of yours. You may find your inheritance somewhat confusing and as such, the second part of the chest's contents are a series of diary entries by Fabrice Charcot, who was present for the end of Nathalie's life. Hopefully these diary entries will answer any questions you might have.

If anything remains unanswered, please do not hesitate to either telephone me at my office, or visit in person. Congratulations on your inheritance, Mme. Beauclaire.

Yours sincerely,
M. Camille Rossignol

As soon as she'd finished reading the letter, she immediately picked up the key. She placed it in the lock, and paused for a moment. The letter had spoken about safety; what on earth could be so dangerous? Soon curiosity won out, however, and she turned the key.

Inside was a folder stuffed with parchment pages filled with cramped, spidery handwriting. Beneath this was a quill pen with a blood red feather and a tip of glittering black metal, a small bottle of dark ink, a walnut-handled straight razor, and a leather-bound book covered in strange, twisting symbols. Effie traced her fingers over the surface of the book and felt a shudder tear through her body.

The hairs on the back of her neck began to rise as her arms

turned to goose-flesh. She shivered despite the summer warmth, and took a step back away from the chest. Her heart was racing slightly and she felt a strange tingling sensation behind her eyes.

She took a deep breath, snatched up the folder, and slammed the chest shut. Once the key was turned and the lock clicked into place, she started to feel a little bit better. What on earth was that all about? She looked down, realising that she was holding the folder so tightly that she threatened to tear it apart.

She decided to pause, make another cup of coffee as the first had grown strangely cold, and take stock. Maybe reading the diary entries was the best course of action after all. She settled into a slightly threadbare armchair with her coffee and started to decipher the untidy scrawl.

August 8th, 1788.
Today I arrived in Saint Denis along with my erstwhile feline companion, Jean-Oddly, ready to begin the next chapter of my life. I'd forgotten how odd it is to be a stranger in a new town! Such sights and sounds that are mundane to the local man are fresh delights to me, the outsider. There have been whispers and rumours of revolution and change for some weeks now, but I neither believe it or care. What can a newly qualified lawyer do to change the world, really?

August 9th, 1788.
My new home, whilst spacious and comfortable, has a certain emptiness to it. Oh, it is not for lack of furniture nor light; you might even call my cottage cluttered. There's an absence of soul in the place, as if the very walls have broken hearts. I only noticed it at the very edge of sleep last night, but now that I'm aware of it, I can no longer pay it no mind.

But all this talk of sullen architecture is not what I meant to note today; I met someone at the market. He was a well-toned man with a tussle of black hair and a well kept beard; he was pale as porcelain, clad all in cream and black, and moved softly as a ghost. I was counting out apples when one fell from my careless grasp. It was as if time slowed as that shining red orb moved through the air toward the muddy street below; it never landed there, however. This strange man deftly caught my apple in his well-manicured fingertips. His nails were painted an inky black that shimmered slightly in the noonday sun. When he wordlessly handed the apple back to me, his fingertips brushed mine and lingered a little longer than I expected; it was surprising but not unpleasant. On the contrary, the old familiar feelings that I had ignored for so many years began their seductive murmurations once again. My breath caught in my throat as I went to thank him, and he smiled at me. His eyes were a golden brown that was almost amber, and I felt myself starting to fall into them. Then he blinked, nodded his head slightly, and walked away.

Nobody else seemed to look at him, or to see him, even, and he certainly paid them no mind as he walked away from the market. He ignored so many hundreds, and smiled at me. I have not yet eaten that particular apple, but I am certain that it will be the sweetest of all.

He smiled for me.

August 11th, 1788.
There is not much to note. I have begun my work, and it is as expected; only the wealthy have the means for legal counsel. I am contemplating reaching out to some friends in Paris to see if we can arrange a fund to allow the less fortunate access to our services. I feel this would do some lasting good to this town. Oh,

Hymns For The Gallows Part Two

I saw the man again today. He was simply sat in the churchyard, feeding crumbs to the birds.

I stopped to look a little too long, and he saw me; I hurried away, but it felt good to be seen.

August 12th, 1788.

The man was in the churchyard again today. We looked at each other a while, and then I went home.

August 15th, 1788.

It has been raining for three days. I have sequestered myself in my shadowy home to focus on my legal writings and the complaints of the wealthy. It is a tedious bore, truth be told, but it puts money in my pocket so I must persevere. My only respite comes in the evenings when, in the pale lamplight, I divulge my thoughts to this diary and my imagination is allowed to wander. I-

Hark, there is someone at the door! Strange, at this hour and in such weather too. I will resume this entry shortly.

August 15th, 1788, later...

Forgive my uneven writing; my hands are still trembling with surprise. When I went to my door to answer the insistent knocking I found no other than the man from the market! It was curious to see him there, smiling softly, with an umbrella in one hand (I've always seen them as more of a Parisian affectation) and a small paper box in the other. All my sense seemed to leave me and I stood back from the threshold and gestured for this smiling stranger to enter my home. He inclined his head and stepped out of the rain, collapsing his umbrella as he did so. He stood to one side as I closed the door, and handed me the little paper box.

"For you," he said softly. It was the first time I'd heard his voice, and it was enchanting. He was from across the sea, from the north of England, and he spoke with a soft, lilting accent. I opencd the box, and inside was a single ornately decorated cake.

We sat quietly by the fireside as I ate his gift, and he smiled at me the whole time; I've never seen teeth glitter and shine as his do. The cake was delicious, with blackberries and fresh cream, and once I had finished he reached out to me and softly wiped a stray speck of cream from at the corner of my mouth. His fingers were surprisingly cold to touch, but my cheeks flushed hot and red.

He left not long afterwards, and I stood in the doorway a while, with Jean-Oddly sat at my feet, both of us watching the rain.

His name is Elijah.

August 20th, 1788.

Elijah and I went walking this evening, through the churchyard. Neither of us said much, and Jean-Oddly took up his usual place upon my shoulder as we strolled in silence. A few of the local townsfolk gave us sideways looks, but I paid them no mind; as long as I have Elijah by my side I have no other wants nor cares in the world.

August 23rd, 1788.

I must apologise again for my skewed writing; I am in a state of shock. Tonight, after walking once more through the churchyard, I invited Elijah home with me; I hoped to make love to him. Instead, as we sat beside the fireplace, he confessed that he had kept a dark secret from me, and that he feared I would no longer wish to spend time with him if he revealed it to me.

I told him that he needn't fear such a thing, not from me, and that he did not need to tell me anything that he did not want to. He smiled, almost tearfully, and kissed me in his chaste, shy way.

"Nobody understands me, Fabrice, and I'm worried that you won't either," he said. I took him in my arms and assured him that was not the case. We spoke around the point a while longer, with his confidence growing, and he suddenly blurted it out, as if the truth would be less shocking if he came upon it by surprise.

"I'm a vampire."

"A what?"

He went on to explain that he is cursed, or indeed blessed, with immortality as long as he consumes the living blood of other people. Sunlight makes him weak, and there are certain odd conventions and rules that he must observe, such as being invited across the threshold of a home, but otherwise he is a normal man with a man's wants and desires.

After telling me all of this, he closed his eyes and waited patiently for me to respond; for me to scream, yell, or demand him to leave, I assume. Instead I took him into my arms and let him weep.

August 24th, 1788.

"How old are you, Elijah?"

"I," he paused for a moment, frozen in place. "I'm not sure. The immortality of body and mind are not intertwined; I don't remember much of my early life. I've outlived so many, and forgotten so much."

August 25th, 1788.

"Doesn't it get lonely?" I asked him.

We avoided the churchyard today.

August 26th, 1788.

This evening I asked Elijah how one even becomes a vampire. He replied that there are two ways; the first, that simply makes a person or animal a shade, and the more involved, intimate method that makes one a full fledged vampire.

A shade is, as far as he remembers, a creature held on the border between life and death. A shade cannot be destroyed and it isn't truly alive either; animals are well suited to being shades as they are freed from their suffering and base needs. Most will apparently gain some intelligence through the process too, if Elijah is to be believed. To make a human a shade, however, is an awful thing; he wouldn't tell me why.

A full vampire can only be born by mingling the flesh, blood, and soul of a mortal with that of a vampire in a ritual that is, by the sounds of it, both tremendously intimate and incredibly violent. I don't wish to read into mere glances too much, but Elijah looked at me with an intensity that was both exhilarating and terrifying as he told me this.

Long have I feared the slow mockery of age or the debilitating spiral of lingering illness; immortality has been a fantasy of mine ever since I was barely in my teens. The loss of my entire family, save my half sister, Nathalie, at a young age gave me a powerful sense of how desperately fragile my own body is.

I won't deny that the lure of vampirism has been on my mind these past few nights.

August 28th, 1788.
This evening as we walked through the twilight, I broached the topic of Elijah bestowing his blessing upon me. He was silent for a time, before quietly telling me that the change can be unpredictable; no two vampires are alike.

The mood between us was a sombre one; I head to Paris for two weeks in the morning. Elijah has kindly agreed to watch my house and Jean-Oddly for me. I hate to be away from them both, but I must put food on the table and I am needed in court.

102

Elijah said that he will think on my request whilst I am gone.

September 13th, 1788.

I have neglected my writing for a few days; it has been eventful since my return from the city. Upon my return three evenings ago I went straight home to find Elijah in a state of distress; apparently someone had thrown a stone at my beloved cat. Poor Jean-Oddly was in a state of awful distress, mewling and screeching in pain. I was distraught, but I have loved him these past five years and I refused to see him suffer; I gathered my resolve and prepared to end his misery.

Elijah stopped me, thankfully, and quietly took him out of the room. I went to follow, but he bade me to sit and wait. I cannot rightly say exactly what he did to my dear companion, but upon their return Jean-Oddly was completely healed.

To be sure, he was his usual scruffy self to the untrained eye, but I have known him his entire life; never before had I seen the swagger that now coloured his walk, nor the mischievous twinkle that graced his amber eyes.

"Did you-?"

"Yes." He closed the distance between us and kissed me, hard. My hips rose to meet his, and we collapsed backwards on to the couch. Both of us were overcome with need and desire; there was nothing shy or chaste about our lovemaking. Jean-Oddly politely left the room; an act so out of character for a raggedy tomcat that it almost distracted me from Elijah.

Almost.

Laying together in the afterglow of our passion Elijah agreed to my request. Tomorrow I am to become a vampire.

I am excited, but not a little afraid.

September 14ᵗʰ, 1788.

It is late, and Elijah suggested that I write in the morning, but I want to capture the details of my ascension whilst they are still fresh in my mind.

We began at sundown. Elijah advised that I should avoid food all day and only drink water; by the time of the ritual I was famished. We stood naked before each other; he is truly a beautiful man with his alabaster skin and thick black curls. We stood mere inches from each other. The tension in the air was palpable as our fingertips lightly brushed together; I must have looked worried.

"Are you afraid?" he asked me.

"Yes," I answered quietly. He leaned closer to me, his mouth by my ear. I shivered a little.

"Do you want me to stop?" I thought before replying; my last chance to walk away.

"No."

It was scarcely a heartbeat later that his razor-sharp teeth sank into my throat. I could feel the yielding resistance of my skin at first, but then the tension was released with an almost audible pop and my lifeblood flowed forth. The pain was indescribable and I tried to scream; all I managed was a weak gurgle as I choked on my own blood.

My knees grew weak as Elijah lowered me to the floor. I felt unconsciousness tugging at the edges of my vision but I fought hard to stay awake; if the blackness took me I knew that I would perish. As my blood poured out of my body my extremities grew cold and trembled uncontrollably. I felt my darling Elijah climb astride me and press the walnut handle of the silver steel straight razor into my palm.

I brought my heavy hand across my torso and with almost herculean effort I flashed the shining blade across my lover's exposed neck. His blood bubbled forth in uncertain rivulets; my cut was not deep, but it was enough. I opened my mouth and let his crimson gift flow on to my expectant tongue and down my parched throat.

As those first hot red droplets entered my body, I came to life. Like a man possessed I rose up to meet Elijah and I drank deeply of his immortal blood. I felt the change start deep in the twisted depths of my body, rising like steam screaming through a pipe; all the colours of my vision deepened, every scent grew richer, and even the grain of the wooden floor was profoundly sensual.

I felt a strange sensation in my mouth, and leant my head to one side; my mortal's teeth fell clattering to the ground in a soft spattering of Elijah's blood. There was a moment of excruciation and ecstasy as the change finally consumed the last of my humanity; in the shuddering afterglow I ran my tongue over my new vampire's fangs. Elijah brought me to my feet, and walked me to the mirror so that I might behold myself.

Bloodied and wild eyed, I scarcely recognised myself; my eyes were aglow with more life than they'd ever had, although a deathly pallor had set into my otherwise rosy cheeks. My new teeth were sharp, shining, and magnificent. My stomach growled with painful hunger.

"You need to feed, my love." We dressed and headed out into the night, and the darkness, that had once held fear for me, now fits me like a second skin.

Tonight I became a vampire.

I will not record the details of that first feeding; it was not a pretty sight.

Elijah waits in my bed for my return, and Jean-Oddly sits upon my desk as I write; never before has a cat looked so judgemental. It is as if he can see the very colour of my soul.

Tonight I killed a person for the first time.

September 29th, 1788.
Something is very wrong.

The vampiric elegance that Elijah carries with him has not manifested itself in me. Instead, I grow more grim and gaunt with each passing day. My skin is pulled tight over my bones and my eyes are sunken and sallow; I look more undead than immortal. My hunger grows more violent with each setting of the sun; there is talk of a serial killer here in Saint Denis. The closeness between Elijah and I has already brought suspicion down upon us.

If they were to see me looking like this...

September 30th, 1788.
Jean-Oddly spoke to me today, albeit briefly. His words were sharp, to be sure, but he seems genuinely concerned for my condition. No matter how much I clean and dust my house it is cluttered with cobwebs as soon as I leave the room. Huge spiders and rats scuttle at the corners of my eyes, tormenting me with their insidious movement; Jean-Oddly pounced upon one and it simply crumbled to grave dirt. Carrion crows tap on the glass of my windows all throughout the day.

I rounded on Elijah and demanded to know what was happening to me. He seemed genuinely sad when he replied.

"The change takes each of us differently, Fabrice. Whilst I have an immortal body and a mortal memory, it seems that you are cursed with the grave; however this likely means that your mind will last forever. Take heart in that at least, my love."

October 1st, 1788.
I demanded that Elijah undo what he has done to me.
He says that he cannot.

106

October 2ⁿᵈ, 1788.

I have, upon the advice of my cat of all things, sent for my half-sister Nathalie; she is a strange woman who lives alone in the countryside. She knows a great deal about a great many things. I have heard her called a witch on more than one occasion and she certainly leans into that title. If anyone can help me, it is her.

If she leaves immediately, she can be here in three days; I hope she does not tary. The mood in Saint Denis grows violent.

Elijah has shut himself in the bedroom and will not talk to me.

October 5ᵗʰ, 1788.

Nathalie arrived this morning, dressed with all the eccentricity that one would expect of a self-declared witch. If the eyes of the town were not already upon us, they are now. I fear that none of us can remain safely in Saint Denis for much longer.

October 6ᵗʰ, 1788.

Nathalie believes that she might have found the answer to my problems; it will be a difficult and bloody ritual, once again, but if it restores me to full life it will be worth it. Elijah has returned to his own home to pack his belongings.

Once the ritual is complete, we are all three of us skipping town. I have had enough of Saint Denis and its Gothic churchyard to last a lifetime. I have only my journal to pack; we complete the ritual at sundown.

October 7ᵗʰ, 1788.

I write this on the road to Paris, in the chilly dawn light. Nathalie's ritual seems to have worked, but at a terrible cost.

We went to the churchyard at sundown; thankfully we met nobody on the way. Nathalie had paid a gravedigger for a coffin and a shallow grave; with enough coin in hand, questions will not be asked. My pack was thrown into the coffin, and I removed my clothes. Nathalie took a vial of my blood and mixed it with a blend of foul smelling herbs and grave dirt before combining it with lampblack and vitriol to make a crimson ink.

She began tracing intricate lines, whorls, and symbols all over my body with her witch's quill, muttering spells from her grimoire as she did so. Once all of these arcane tattoos were complete, she instructed me to stand on the edge of the grave, and looked at me sadly.

"I'm sorry, Fabrice," she whispered, before driving her quill deep into my heart. I fell backwards into the coffin as fire spread through my veins. I wanted to writhe in pain, to scream in agony, but I was limp as a corpse. She placed her grimoire at my feet, along with the ink, before nailing the coffin lid shut. I could only lie there as my own sister buried me alive.

It was not long after that I heard some commotion above, muffled by the loose soil. That soon died down, and I was left with the silence and my own thoughts. After yet more time still, the sensation returned to my body and I realised the lid was barely held in place by the nails and that no more than four inches of soil were above me.

I dragged myself out of my shallow grave and knelt there in the pre-dawn mists; the only sound was the soft creaking of a rope. It was only as my senses acclimatised that I realised the mist was tinged with the smell of smoke, and that the eerie sound came from above me.

Slowly, tentatively, I turned to look upwards.

Nathalie swung from a sturdy branch in the tree above me; the first hanging of a witch in Saint Denis in almost a hundred years. I was about to scream when I saw Jean-Oddly looking down at me.

"Gather your wits and then your belongings, Fabrice. Your home is burned and your lover has fled; we would be wise to do the same. Do not leave Nathalie's implements behind; they may yet be useful. The sun will soon be up. Do not weep and do not tary. Come along!"

And here I find myself; on the road to a life unknown with naught but the clothes on my back, the belongings in my pack, and a talking cat that only I can hear.

At least I look like an ordinary man again; Nathalie's death was not in vain.

October 7th, 1788, later...
I am in a state of shock.

I was attacked by a ruffian on the road. He demanded my pack and I refused; I expected a brawl, but was surprised when he drew a pistol and shot me. His aim was true and the bullet hit me squarely in the chest.

I felt pain, but nowhere near as much as I should have. I put a hand to my chest and it came away wet; not with blood, but with ink. I blinked as this registered in my brain, then drew my razor from my pocket.

My assailant tried to draw a blade, but I was too fast for him. I am a practised throat-cutter after all, and I quickly took his life. As he lie on the ground, the old hunger took me, and I drank deeply of his blood; it was not the same primal need as before, but it was still invigorating.

It was only after I drank his body dry that I realised the truth.

I finally have the immortality I wanted.

May 18th, 1927.
I have not looked in this journal for almost one hundred and forty years. I have led many lives, fought in many wars, and

killed many people in that time. I've buried lovers and enemies alike; I can call each and every one of their faces to mind. The only constant in my life is my damnable, if reliable cat, Jean-Oddly. We are two immortals in a world of fools hurtling towards the grave.

I wish I could say that I did not know why I opened this journal today, but that would be a lie. This morning, in the papers, I saw an article by a relative of Nathalie's; in the dimness of my mind I knew that she had a child, but not once did I think to seek them out to clear her name.

Perhaps I will engineer a chance meeting with this Rosaline Beauclaire; it isn't like I've much else to do.

March 5th, 1961.

I am so desperately tired of life. Even the drinking of hot, fresh blood is pedestrian now. A not insignificant part of me hopes for the so-called Nuclear Holocaust that the papers speak of so often; surely in the atomic fires of Armageddon, I will at last have some god damn peace.

February 11th, 1987.

I ran into Elijah in a bar in Soho, whilst he was chatting up some attractive young thing; all blonde hair and bleached teeth. I couldn't believe that I'd found him again, after almost two hundred years! When the object of his desire went to the bar, I decided to speak to him.

It's true what he said about the trade-off of an immortal body. He doesn't remember me.

October 19th, 2003.

I never thought I'd see Paris again; I've not been back here since the Revolution. I've changed my name to Camille Rossignol and founded a legal practice. I've had several lifetimes to hone my craft, after all, and there's a pleasing symmetry about all of it; I feel like I've come full circle.

January 8th, 2021.

The rise of the internet is something that I never expected. There are cameras everywhere, and facial recognition software makes existing as an immortal an increasingly risky business; I do not want to get spirited away by some shadowy government agency to be experimented on for all eternity.

My colleagues have started asking how I continue to look so youthful; I throw out whatever health trend is currently all the rage, and that seems to mollify them. Sometimes, if I'm feeling impish, I tell them that it's the blood of the youthful; a habit I still indulge from time to time. They also gently mock me for using a typewriter instead of a computer; I just quietly say that I've a special connection with good old-fashioned ink.

Which, of course, is true.

But I am so very tired, Effie. I've been watching your family for generations now, searching for the perfect person to tell my story and bequeath my sister's tools to; that search is now over. You have Nathalie's talents, that much is certain, and I give you my blessing to use them as you see fit.

I do have one small favour to ask of you, however.

If your travels should ever bring you through Paris, please look me up. We can go for a drink, I can fill in any gaps in my story you might want to hear, and then you can kill me. Please don't feel pressured to rush on over, though; all at your convenience.

After all, I've got nothing but time.

Eleanor Fitzgerald

A Note from the Writer, Part II

You'll notice that the tone of this anthology is a bit different from the previous one, dear reader. This one is a lot bloodier, a lot raunchier, and, truth be told, a lot more transgender positive.

I had a little bit of a wobble back in January/February time and I realised that I had internalised *a lot* of transphobia; it was starting to colour my thoughts about myself and it was genuinely undermining my happiness.

Thankfully, I've started to pull that shit out of my head and I'm in a better place for it. Not a perfect place, to be sure, but a better one. I won't elaborate here, but if you read on to the *Digestif*, you can find some further details.

So, are you sick of my voice yet?

No? Well, that's kind of you to say. You might have started to notice that there are some recurring themes within my writing, especially if you read Volume One.

I discussed these themes with some friends, and we settled on the thirteen fundamentals of my writing; my poems and stories will always contain at least one of the follow, but often multiple.

Horniness, Vampirism, Rage, Horror, Irreverence, Sorrow, Cannibalism, Anti-Capitalism, Gender Stuff, Trauma, Science, Culture/Heritage, and References to Pop Culture; some of these tend to come in pairs or groups. I have decided that a poem that contains all of these things will not necessarily be the best poem I ever write, but certainly the *most* poem I could create.

And, if you wish to see more from this grab bag of themes, and to read the conclusion of Dark's story, please join me again in:

Hymns for the Gallows, Volume Three: The Hanging

Hymns For The Gallows Part Two

<u>Acknowledgements</u>

Another one finished, and as always I couldn't have done any of this without the help of those around me. I have several people that I'd like to thank in particular for helping me get this far.

Firstly, my partner Thomas Robertson, who has encouraged my writing and creativity since day one, and whose love has been a lighthouse in uncertain seas. Next, my dear friend Anna Sturrock, whom I love very much and has given me a wealth of both inspiration and counsel during the compiling of this anthology; as a colleague of mine used to say, you shine like a shaft of gold when all around is dark. My metamour, Ineke, for all of her support and the smiles that she's brought into my life. My close friend Dr Georgia Lynott, who always brings light and laughter to my day. Next, Serin Gioan who I will shamelessly blame for the sheer quantity of vampire themed content in this anthology. Nicola Courtier, for kindly allowing me to share the rewrite of Blood and Ink with you all. Once again, Zayna Ratty, my therapist, whose excellent life advice has allowed me to focus on the creative parts of my soul rather than the endlessly self-destructive. Jamie Cameron esq. and Wesley McKean esq. for introducing me to the concept of cold welding, which inspired the poem of the same name. My friend Karen, who sat and chatted with me to help me focus on actually putting words on the page. My friends Emma Mellene Bokaldere and Peter John Stafford, for both their wonderful presence in my life and a stimulating December conversation around a roaring fire. Janet and Josie Bond for taking me in during that rainy December when I had nowhere else to go. The Qu-h-ear Voices community for once again providing so much support for my writing and a place to read my poems publicly.

I'd also like to thank all the other Parrots that I don't have time to mention explicitly by name; you are all in my heart and never far out of mind.

And, as always, you, my dear reader.

Thank you.

<u>Digestif</u>

Well, well, well; here we are again, dear reader. The permission that I gave you last time to scribble, scrawl, and doodle in the blank spaces of this publication still stands; by all means, have at.

I want to say something personal to you now, however. That little caveat about not reading into things drops here, because I'm going to explicitly talk about myself for once.

I'm going to talk to you about suicide.

I know it's unpleasant, but please bear with me here; it's important to me.

A lot of my artistic idols and inspirations have taken their own lives; Sylvia Plath and Vincent Van Gogh, to name but two. I've lost people close to me too. Suicide has been a pervasive part of my life for a very, very long time.

I've tried to take my own life a number of times; the most recent was (at time of writing) Saturday April 13th, 2019. Whilst I haven't made an attempt since then, I've thought about it every single day. Themes of suicide are rife in my writing because it's a part of my everyday life.

This isn't because I'm in the depths of a mental health crisis; in fact, my life is going better than I ever thought possible. I think about, and indeed plan out, my suicide every single day because it's an option and it's my decision to make; it's one of the few things I have total and complete agency over. The other is my writing.

Every single day, often unbidden, I find myself weighing my options and the reasons for each, and let me tell you that the smallest fucking thing can tip the scales in favour of life. The little things really do give me something to live for but sometimes they count for naught; it's a crap-shoot as to what will matter on any given day.

So far, the coin has come up life every single toss since that awful Saturday, although it has been a close-cut thing more often than I'd care to admit. Right now, in this moment, I do want to keep on living. That doesn't mean that I'll stop considering my options, however; this state of almost perpetual suicidality is likely to exist for the rest of my life.

So, that's all very well and good, but why on earth am I telling you this?

Well, the reasons are twofold. Firstly, should I ever take my own life, which I currently have no plans to do, please know that there was nothing you could have done; it was my choice, and my agency means more than anything to me. I'll say it one more time, for those in the back; I currently do not want to take my own life. This is all just in case.

Secondly, and this is the main reason, I know that I can't be the only one. There are surely other folks out there that go through the same thing, and I want them to know that they're not alone. I want them to know that it doesn't make you any less of a person, nor does it make your art any less valuable, nor do you deserve life any less, and fuck anyone that says otherwise.

I know that it is often quite obvious when I'm struggling with my suicidal urges; I get a thousand yard stare or start crying. If this happens and I happen to be in your presence, please don't tell me what I have to live for, or how my suicide will impact others, or try to influence my decision at all; it won't make a lick of difference.

Instead, if I say that I'm feeling suicidal all you need to say is "Wow, that sounds pretty shit. You want a cup of tea?" That's it, and that will almost always make a difference. I know it's only a little thing, but knowing that I'm not alone as I ride out those difficult moments weighing up life and death make the whole thing so much more bearable.

I guess the small things count more than I realise. Anyway, dear reader, I do apologise for bringing up such an uncomfortable subject, but I felt that it was important.

Until next time, my friend.

Lots of love,
Eleanor xxxx

Eleanor Fitzgerald

About the Author

Eleanor Fitzgerald (she/they) was born under a vastly different name just outside London in 1992. She grew up in Cornwall, for the most part, and has a deep affinity for the ocean. She studied Chemistry at Trinity College, Oxford, between 2010 and 2015. Eleanor came out as a Non-Binary Transgender Woman in the summer of 2014, after much soul-searching.

Whilst she has professionally worked in science since 2015, she describes herself as having "the soul of an artist", with a passion for prose, poetry, sculpture, and painting. Eleanor practices Judaism, and is disabled; she walks with a walking stick due to chronic pain. She describes herself as 'Queer' and sits on the Asexual spectrum. She is ethically non-monogamous. Eleanor is a drag artist, and performs under the name Ayn Randy.

If you'd like to get in touch with any questions, comments, and queries you can reach Eleanor at:

EleanorFitzgeraldWriting@gmail.com.

Printed in Great Britain
by Amazon